Leon the Lion

This book belongs to

_____

Leon the Lion's Bad Day

How this story came to be...

When Amanda was sixteen, she went to the kitchen to ask her mother a question. Engaged in doing housework, Mom happened not to be in a good mood at that moment, and was rather short with Amanda. Amanda left the kitchen and went to her room, momentarily saddened by the encounter. But rather than sulk and fume, she took pen to paper and expressed her feelings by writing an animal story, the poem that became *Leon the Lion*.

Leon the Lion's Bad Day

by Amanda Franken

Illustrated by David Wentworth

Leon the Lion was
Stuck in a rut,
Cooped up on the bed
Inside of his hut.

He sat by himself
All gloomy and glum
He made not a sound,
As if he were dumb.

The animals met
At the old jungle gym.

They thought and they talked
About how to help him.

"I think Leon's dying,"
Said old Billy Bear.

"Or perhaps he is losing
All of his hair."

Said Ronald Raccoon,
"No, that can't be right.
Leon's in a bad mood –
Can't you see that's his plight?

"I say we give him
About half a day.
I bet that his grumpiness
Soon goes away."

But the grumpiness stayed,
And as you may know
When grumpiness stays,
It often will grow.

Leon started to whimper,
Sniffle and pout.
He hid in his bedroom
And wouldn't come out.

So the others agreed
They would cheer Leon up.

The first one to try was
Petunia the Pup.

She offered Leon
His favorite dish:

Roasty, toasty, salted
Cat-whiskered fish.

Leon the Lion
Turned up his nose,

And Leon the Lion
Curled up his toes.

Petunia felt awful.
She started to cry,

So then Bella Bunny
Decided to try.

Bella had puppets
Of three little pigs

    All dressed up in blouses
    And curly blond wigs.

To cheer up poor Leon,
She put on a show.
Then Leon's furry face –
It started to glow!

But alas, when the evil wolf
Blew the house down,
Leon the Lion
Returned to his frown.

As Bella joined Petunia
On the rejected seat,

On came comic canary,
Jacques de le Tweet.

He told several jokes —
Of immature taste —

And dignified Leon

Punched him square in the face.

Finally, after some
Two thousand tries,

The animals sat there
With tears in their eyes.

"We tried and we failed,"
Said a housefly named Bob.

They all came together
And started to sob.

Such horrible wailing –
They fussed and they cried.

Leon heard the commotion
And sprang out from inside.

He saw them all bawling
And then he said, "Hey!

Is that how *I've* been
Behaving all day?"

Then Leon surprised them,
With a big lion smile,

"I'm all cheered up now!
It just took me a while!"

And then they were happy!
Such laughter! Such joy!

And now here's the lesson
For each girl and boy:

It's all right to be sad –
But don't forget to get glad,
Because, in a hurry,
All your best friends will worry.

ABOUT THE AUTHOR

Amanda Franken grew up with a lifelong love of books and reading. Diagnosed at age five with Asperger's Syndrome, it certainly hasn't inhibited her as an avid writer of short stories and campfire stories. She also enjoys cartooning, and her fondness for animals has become an integral part of her storytelling. You can find more of her work on Writing.com (under the name Twiga) and FanFiction.net.

Amanda grew up and lives with her family in Southern California. She has one younger sister, Stephanie.

ABOUT THE ILLUSTRATOR

Artist and illustrator David Wentworth graduated from the Massachusetts College of Art in Boston and later the Academy of Art University in San Francisco, receiving both his BFA and MFA with a focus in illustration. When not telling his own stories or the tales of others, he also makes puppets and works in a wide variety of mediums and tools.

Originally from Massachusetts, growing up around the woods and wetlands of New England gave David an early passion for wildlife and for the adventures, experiences, and perspectives of living creatures in all their diversely evolved forms. Story telling is a core aspect of his work, using scientific themes to give it a believable strength, despite it perhaps being whimsical fiction. His work often skirts the line between playful and serious, both in mood and style.

To see more of his artwork, ask your parent or guardian for permission to visit his website at DavidWentworthArt.com.

ACKNOWLEDGMENTS

James Franken, Producer (and Amanda's father), who after reading Amanda's poem replete with all its vivid images, was inspired to share her work with the world by creating this children's book. With no experience in the world of book-making or publishing, he embarked on a two-year journey, culminating in this book, *Leon the Lion's Bad Day*.

The Producer wishes to graciously thank Beth Franken, PhD (Amanda's aunt), who edited Amanda's original text. Her insights were most helpful. Also, Stephanie Franken (Amanda's sister) added key contributions and improvements.

Thank you so much to David Wentworth, Illustrator, who spent inordinate amounts of time creating and refining the artwork for his first children's book, with painstaking detail applied to the characters and background. From start to finish, David was a pleasure to work with, always open to comment and suggestion. David quickly grasped the vision of what Leon the Lion was about. His characters embody the spirit of the text, and helped create a story with a thoughtful message that parents can share with their children.